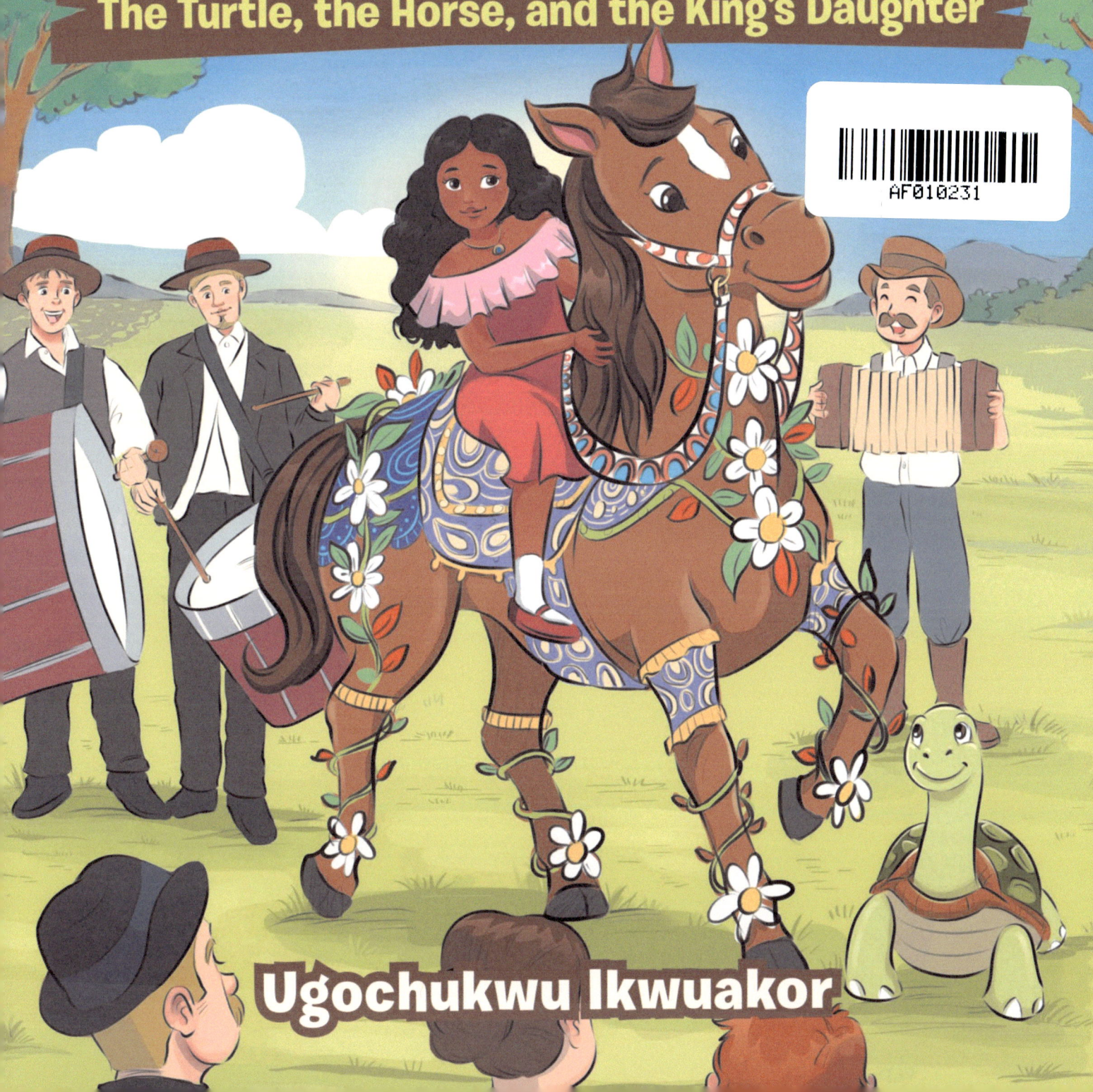

SHARING YOUR ABILITY

The Turtle, the Horse, and the King's Daughter

Why People Ride on Horses

*People are talented in one form or another.
How well they use that talent is what counts.*

Ugochukwu Ikwuakor
Illustrated by Shannen Marie Paradero

Copyright © 2024 **Ugochukwu Ikwuakor Publishing**

All rights reserved. No part of this publication may be reproduced, distributed, or transmitted in any form or by any means, including photocopying, recording, or other electronic or mechanical methods, without the prior written permission of the publisher, except in the case of brief quotations embodied in critical reviews and certain other noncommercial uses permitted by copyright law. For permission requests, write to the publisher, addressed "Attention: Book Rights and Permission," at the address below.

Published in the United States of America

ISBN 978-1-961507-28-9 (SC)
ISBN 979-8-89395-075-5 (HC)
ISBN 979-8-89395-935-2 (Ebook)

Ugochukwu Ikwuakor Publishing
222 West 6th Street
Suite 400, San Pedro, CA, 90731
www.stellarliterary.com

Order Information and Rights Permission:

Quantity sales. Special discounts might be available on quantity purchases by corporations, associations, and others. For details, contact the publisher at the address above.

For Book Rights Adaptation and other Rights Permission. Call us at toll-free 1-888-945-8513 or send us an email at admin@stellarliterary.com.

Once upon a time in a village called Amanta, word spread out that the king's first daughter, Ada, was sad and refused even to smile. Normally she was friendly and kind to everyone, and she appeared every day at the village square to help the poor and the elderly. She smiled all the time and enjoyed being with the people.

When the villagers heard that Ada was unhappy, they became worried and wondered what was going on. They had not seen the princess in nearly two weeks, and there was a rumor that Ada was sick and might not be out again. Some villagers went to the palace to find out about Ada.

The king also became concerned about his daughter and called his entire family for a meeting. At the meeting, he asked Ada, "Why are you not happy?"

"I don't know," she replied. "I just don't feel happy anymore."

"Can I make you happy like this?" asked Obi, Ada's younger sister, with her two hands on her waist and twisting her hips.

"Or like this?" asked Ada's brother, Chidi, who folded his arms behind his back, lay down, and tried to move on his stomach.

Ada remained silent. Other members of her family performed their own tricks and dance, but nothing made Ada happy.

The king became more worried and even grew angry. He thought his daughter was acting strangely and making her family look bad. The king was well liked and respected by his people, and what was going on in his house bothered him. It was during that year's moon festival, and he hoped that with so many festivities and ceremonies, his daughter would be happy again.

While all these things were going on, Turtle, also known as the wise one, heard about the king and his daughter and decided to go to the palace. Early the next day, he left his home to visit the king's palace, a journey that took him all day.

When he arrived, he knocked on the garden gate.

"Who is it?" asked the king's gardener

"Me, me," replied Turtle.

The gardener opened the gate but did not see anyone. He looked down and jumped back when he saw Turtle.

"The wise one?" the gardener shouted. "What are you doing here?"

"I'm here to see the king," Turtle answered.

"Wait."

The gardener rushed inside, came back, and invited Turtle in. He led Turtle to the king, who was sitting in his chair by the fireplace. Turtle greeted the king and sat down on the small chair the gardener had set out for him.

"What can I do for you, wise one?" the king asked Turtle.

"I heard about Ada, and I came to see what I can do to help," Turtle said.

"Help?" the king asked in a sad voice. "I need help. I have done everything, but nothing worked."

"Do not be discouraged, my king," Turtle said. "I came to tell you that I know someone who can help."

"Who?" asked the king; he quickly got out of his chair and then sat again. "I will do anything to make Ada happy. Who is it? Whoever makes her happy again will be rewarded and will be a prince or princess in my kingdom."

"Be patient, my king," Turtle assured him. "I will be back in seven days, on the next market day."

That very market day was the start of the moon festival that year, when the king invited the musicians, dancers, magicians, and clowns to his palace to celebrate. The moon festival usually lasted for three days. It was a holiday, and everyone celebrated and didn't work.

Turtle said goodbye to the king and left the palace. On his way back to his home, Turtle went to visit his friend Horse. It was Horse whom he had in mind for helping the king and his daughter. Horse was a magician, and Turtle had seen him dance and perform his magic on several occasions. To Turtle, Horse was the best dancer and magician in the whole wild world.

It was springtime, when people, especially farmers, got ready for the start of the farming season. On that cloudy day, Horse was in the field near his home, galloping with his friends.

"Good day, my friend," Turtle shouted when he saw Horse.

"Wise one!" Horse shouted back and ran to Turtle. "What are you doing here?"

"I went to see the king and his daughter and then came by to see you," Turtle answered.

"I heard what is going on there. How is she?" Horse asked.

"I did not see Ada, but I promised the king I knew someone who could help," Turtle replied.

"Who?" Horse anxiously asked.

"Y-y-y-y-y-y-you," Turtle stammered.

"Me?" Horse said.

"My good friend," Turtle continued, "I have known you for a long time and have seen you dance and do your magic. You are better than anyone out there, and I know you can make the girl smile and be happy again. The king is a good man; please let us help him."

"How?" Horse asked Turtle.

"You and I are invited as the king's guests next market day," Turtle said. "You know it is the start of the moon festival, and different groups are invited to the palace. The king said that whoever can make his daughter happy again will be the prince of the palace. Hopefully the king will make us the princes of his kingdom."

"I would like to go," said Horse. "But how can we be the princes of the kingdom? We won't be able to do anything for the king."

"Don't worry," Turtle assured Horse. "Wait for me early on the morning of market day. We will try to be at the palace on time for the festival at noon."

"See you then," said Horse.

Early in the morning on market day, Horse was ready and waiting for Turtle. But when hours went by and there was no sign of Turtle, Horse became worried.

He waited and waited and waited. He was already losing hope about going to the palace when Turtle finally showed up. By that time, it was almost midday.

"Wise one," Horse stated, with dejection in his voice, "we are very late, and we won't get the chance to see the king again."

"No, we will see the king," Turtle quickly assured Horse. "I had to rush to see my sick grandma early this morning, and that's why I am late. Let's go."

The two friends left for the king's palace. The journey was far, and they were already late. Horse became anxious and wanted to walk faster, but because of Turtle's slowness, he had to walk more slowly. Horse was not very happy and started murmuring to himself.

"Did you say something?" Turtle asked Horse. Horse did not reply but kept on walking.

Turtle sensed that his good friend was not happy. "You know I cannot walk as quickly as you can," said Turtle. "If you let me climb on your back, you can run fast, and maybe we can make it on time."

"Why didn't I think about that before?" said Horse, turning around to face Turtle. "Please, please jump on my back."

He lowered himself, and Turtle climbed on his back. Instantly Horse raced toward the village of Amanta as fast as he could. They reached the palace way past noon. By then the ceremony was winding down, and people leaving the palace showed no smiles on their faces.

"What happened? Why are you leaving?" Turtle asked a group of people at the gate to the palace.

"Nothing happened," they replied. "No one made Ada happy."

"Go in," Turtle ordered Horse.

With Turtle still on his back, Horse rushed in, ignoring the shouts of the guard to stop. He galloped into the palace, and people screamed and gave way when they saw him. The music had already stopped. The king and his family were about to go inside, and several other guests were leaving the palace.

"Wait," Turtle shouted, hurriedly climbing down from the back of Horse. The remaining crowd started talking and shouting, and they immediately surrounded Horse and Turtle. The king turned around to see what was going on.

"Move back," Turtle yelled to the crowd. Horse whinnied and raised his forelegs in the air, as if to knock someone. Many in the crowd screamed and were scared. While moving back to make room for Horse, many people fell on the ground; some got up quickly, but others found their hands and feet being trampled.

"Wise one?" the king asked, surprised to see Turtle.

"Yes, my king," Turtle replied. "I promised you I would bring someone to help. This is my good friend Horse, the best dancer and magician in the world. Please bring Ada and others and sit down. My friend will not disappoint you."

The king and his family, as well as other invited guests who had not left the palace, sat down again. Turtle then motioned to the drummers to beat the drums.

"The floor is yours, my friend," Turtle told Horse.

The drums started, the flutes followed, and the gongs played, all in one rhythm. Horse moved to the middle of the floor and started dancing in circles and moving his body to the beat of the music. In an instant, he raised his forelegs, and the music became loud and fast. He brought the forelegs down and continued dancing. In one motion, he stood by his hind legs and raised his forelegs in the air, twisting his waist and going in circles. In another motion, he jumped up and came down, shaking his head from side to side. He looked up in the sky and screamed, spewing a white smoke out from his mouth. He again raised his forelegs in the air and kept them there for a while.

The king clapped, and the others present shouted, cheered, and applauded. The drums became louder and faster. Horse had not finished. Dancing on all four legs, he again shook his head from side to side. His ears became straight and widened, and the shiny hairs on his body rose up. He danced and danced and then majestically moved toward the king and his family. A few feet from the king and directly facing Ada, he stopped dancing, threw his forelegs once more in the air, and clapped his shoes together, making clopping sounds. From nowhere came two beautiful white doves. It was magic.

Seeing the doves, Ada rose from her seat, smiled, yelled in approval, and clapped. The king and all the crowd rose and yelled and clapped too. The crowd yelled and clapped.

Horse clapped his shoes again, and both doves gracefully flew to Ada and rested on her shoulders. Ada opened her hands, and one dove sat on each hand. She smiled and threw them up in the air, and they circled and flew back to her.

Then the king motioned for the music to stop.

"Thank you, my dear friends," he said to Turtle and Horse. "You have done us good. From now on, you are princes in my kingdom and are welcome anytime. Thank you, thank you, and thank you."

Turtle and Horse were about to leave when Ada stopped them.

"Please, can you take me to the market square tomorrow to greet the people?" Ada asked Horse.

Horse looked at Turtle, who nodded.

"Yes, I will take you there tomorrow," Horse replied.

Horse and Turtle stayed in the palace for the night. The next day, when it was time, the palace maids decorated Horse with flowers and ornaments. When Ada was ready, she sat on the decorated Horse. With the musicians, drummers, Turtle, and others following behind, Horse took Ada to the market square to greet the people. It was a colorful celebration, and since then people have been riding on horses.

Printed by Libri Plureos GmbH in Hamburg, Germany